Pinky's Sweet Tooth

Michele Malkin

DUTTON CHILDREN'S BOOKS

New York

For John, who never gains an ounce,
despite his sweet tooth

And a special thanks to SVM

E mal

CIP Data is available.

Published in the United States 2003 by Dutton Children's Books,
a division of Penguin Putnam Books for Young Readers
345 Hudson Street, New York, New York 10014
www.penguinputnam.com
Designed by Richard Amari
Manufactured in China
First Edition
1 3 5 7 9 10 8 6 4 2
ISBN 0-525-47088-3

When most people are still snug under their covers, my Aunt Pinky is already at work, cracking eggs, mixing up batter, and putting funny little shapes of dough into the oven.

Aunt Pinky owns a bakery named Pinky's Sweet Tooth. Her motto is: VEGETABLES CAN WAIT— DESSERT COMES FIRST.

When I'm not at school, I help Aunt Pinky at the bakery. It's not easy getting out of bed before the sun comes up. Sometimes I want to turn off my alarm and go back to sleep. But Aunt Pinky is expecting me, so I get up, brush my teeth, and go right over to the Sweet Tooth.

It's my job to set out the ingredients.

Baking is like magic. You start with some flour, baking powder, and a smidgen of salt. Cream together butter and sugar. Crack some eggs, stir in milk, and add a little vanilla. Mix the whole thing up, pop it in the oven, and presto! Out comes a delicious cake!

"Don't forget the chocolate, Lulu," says Aunt Pinky. "Today we'll need extra. I'm making Chocolate Yummies, Chocolate Bunny Pie, Chocolate Fudge Surprise, Chocolate Coco Cups, and six Triple Chocolate Frenzy Tortes."

Aunt Pinky always asks for extra chocolate.

When Aunt Pinky first opened the Sweet Tooth, things were a little slow. Most people did not know she made the best desserts in town.

There were only a few
regular customers.

Louie dropped in at noon
every day for a slice of fresh
blueberry pie.

Henrietta arrived before
teatime to pick up an assort-
ment of scones.

Daisy came before closing
time. She couldn't live
without the Chocolate
Fudge Surprise.

Still, there were usually
some desserts left over at
the end of the day.

"Don't worry," Aunt Pinky would say. "Fame isn't easy to come by. You have to know what you want, work very hard, and have luck on your side. Without luck on your side, well...then you have to get up really early in the morning."

One Saturday, a bright yellow envelope arrived at the Sweet Tooth. Inside was an invitation to the county fair.

"There's going to be a contest for the Best Dessert in the County," said Aunt Pinky, waving the invitation at me.

"You make the best desserts in the WHOLE UNIVERSE!" I said. "You have to enter the contest!"

"What a wonderful idea!" she exclaimed. "I have to bake something extraordinary! I *must* win this contest!"

By the time we were ready for our cookie break, Aunt
Pinky had thought of not one but *three* possible prizewinners.

"What about my Triple Chocolate Frenzy Torte?" she
said. "Or my Chocolate Coco Cups? Or I could do my
Chocolate Yummies. They're a real crowd-pleaser."

"What about your Chocolate Bunny Pie?" I asked.

"Oh no!" cried Aunt Pinky. "I completely forgot about
my Chocolate Bunny Pie!!!"

Later there was a delay during the afternoon rush. "I'll
be right with you," said Aunt Pinky to a peevish Henrietta.
She was busy searching through her recipe file for the perfect
dessert.

Several days passed, and Aunt Pinky could not decide which dessert to make. She asked her loyal customers for advice.

Louie's first choice was his usual mouthwatering blueberry pie.

Henrietta suggested her personal favorite, the scrumptious huckleberry scone.

Daisy voted for the dessert she couldn't live without, the heavenly Chocolate Fudge Surprise.

They were no help at all.

Aunt Pinky stayed up late, thinking of new desserts. So many of them tempted her sweet tooth, she decided it was time to ask an expert, someone who knew the difference between pretty good and Out of This World.

Someone like *me!*

On Friday afternoon, Aunt Pinky made up a batch of every kind of cake, pie, and cookie she could think of. I poured a glass of cold milk and got right to work. I had narrowed my decision to either a Chocolate Yummie, a Tutti-Frutti Cookie, a Cherry Cheese Dream, or a Chocolate Bunny Pie when Aunt Pinky came out of the kitchen again.

"Lulu, you've got to try these. I just came up with some

new recipes." She was holding a tray piled high with treats, and she was covered in flour from head to tail.

Everything was delicious. Finally, I had to admit that I didn't know which dessert was the yummiest. And I was ready to burst!

What were we going to do? The rules said "One dessert per contestant," and the county fair was TOMORROW!

That night, Aunt Pinky called me at home.

"Lulu, meet me at the dessert booth tomorrow morning," she said.

"What dessert are you making?" I asked.

"I can't talk right now," she replied. "I've got a lot of baking to do!"

The next day, I got to the fair early and went right to the dessert booth. Aunt Pinky was not there yet.

When the mayor arrived, there was still no sign of her.

I wondered where she could be.

The mayor started the judging by sampling a cottage-cheese pie.

The contestants watched eagerly as he worked his way through an oatmeal-prune square, a raisin pound cake, and an orange-marmalade tart. I started to worry. Would Aunt Pinky get here before the contest ended?

The mayor was biting into a sour-cream babka when I finally spotted Aunt Pinky. She was pulling something so huge, people had to get out of the way to let her through.

"Lulu, I've outdone myself this time," she told me when she arrived at the booth.

She unveiled her masterpiece.

"What in the world is *that?*" gasped the mayor.

"I couldn't decide which one of my favorite recipes to make," explained Aunt Pinky. "So I made them *all!* It's a Triple Chocolate Yummie Bunny Coco Fudge Frenzy Torte Surprise!"

The crowd cheered. It was the most wonderful dessert we had ever seen.

Lots of Eats at the Fair

Well, almost everyone cheered. The mayor sniffed loudly and said, "Quiet, please. I have made my decision."

Then he gave the first prize to a teeny, tiny, no-sugar, no-honey, no-fat, no-icing piece of crumb cake with NOT EVEN A BIT OF CHOCOLATE!

I demanded to know why Aunt Pinky had lost.

"There are rules, my dear," the mayor declared. "That looks like more than one dessert to me."

I was all set to give him a piece of my mind when Aunt
Pinky spoke. "Sometimes, Mr. Mayor, to create something
extraordinary, you have to *bend* the rules."

She quickly covered the giant dessert. "Lulu, I know
just the spot for this baby," she said cheerfully.

It wasn't long before everyone heard about Aunt Pinky's giant dessert.

People started coming from all over just to see the Triple Chocolate Yummie Bunny Coco Fudge Frenzy Torte Surprise.

You can't miss it. It's right in front of the enormously popular Pinky's Sweet Tooth.

Just looking at that giant cake makes people hungry.

It's a good thing we have so many yummy desserts to eat.

The only hard part is picking just one!